TRANSLATING GOD FOR KIDS!

GROWING UP with GOD

Everyday adventures of hearing God's voice

BY SHAWN BOLZ

Published by
NewType Publishing
Get Your Words Out
NewTypePublishing.com

Printed in the USA.

ISBN: 978-1-942306-57-3

Illustrations | R.W. Lamont Hunt | www.dakotakidcreations.com
Cover design & interior layout | Yvonne Parks | www.pearcreative.ca

DEDICATION

I dedicate this book to my parents, who helped
me grow up with God and are the inspiration for
this kind of book. I also want to dedicate it to my
family: Cherie, my wife, who has partnered all the
way on this, and my girls, Harper and Hartley,
who are the loves of my life and already have
such an amazing connection to God.

CHAPTER 1

Maria looked around at all of her old friends and all the new friends she'd made in the past week, and she couldn't believe they were in the last night of Lake Christian Summer Camp. It had been so much fun, with the swimming, horseback riding, and relay races . . . but her favorite moment was when her friend Lucas had initiated an innocent s'mores fight at the campfire the night before. Everyone was so sticky, and chocolate-covered faces made for some great pictures.

Maria had also loved the spiritual side of the camp, and she had never felt so connected to music as when she was joining in during the worship times.

It wasn't just about singing songs; it was that it made her feel so present with God. She loved the words everyone was singing, but the worship went beyond words now in her mind. It was an expression of their hearts.

She and her two close camp friends, Lucas and Harper, were standing together worshipping when their children's pastor came up to the front to share.

"It has been a great week, and I had so much fun with you guys. I love that our spiritual focus this year is on friendship with God and hearing His voice. Lucas," the pastor singled him out, "that was an amazing prophetic word the guest speaker gave you on the first night. Because we are in the last night of camp, I want to practice what we have been learning about hearing God's voice. Let's ask God to speak through each other about something specific for this upcoming school year, and we are going to break up into groups of two or three and pray together to do this."

Everyone had felt the buildup of anticipation over the full week of inspirational meetings they had been a part of. Harper ran to pray with her sister, Hartley, which left Lucas with Maria. She

liked Lucas being her partner because he took God
very seriously, and he was also very enjoyable to be
around.

"Have you ever heard God,
Lucas? I mean,
besides that
amazing
prophecy you
got the first
night?" The
assignments
they had been
doing all week
to help them hear
God's voice didn't
feel like they

were working for her very well. A lot of the kids had already shared amazing personal stories of encountering God and getting prophetic revelation. Although she believed she'd soon have stories of her own to share,

she just hadn't had anything happen yet. All the camp instructors had said that friendship with God meant that you could hear His voice, and she hadn't.

"Yeah, He speaks to me a lot," Lucas said.

"How do you know what you are hearing is Him and not you?" Maria twirled a strand of her red hair around her finger.

"Well, He usually tells me things I wasn't already thinking about, or invites me to do things I would never think about doing. Like the other day, when we were at dinner, I felt like I was supposed to take Harper's place to do after-dinner KP [clean up]. I hate KP, but when I asked her if she wanted me to do it, she was so grateful—she'd been invited to be on the worship team that night and needed to be there early for practice. She had just prayed to get out of KP when I asked her if I could take her shift. Me doing a little extra KP helped her get to do something she really loves. I think that when we are always ready to hear God, He helps us do things that help the world around us, even if they're just little things."

Maria nodded. "I wish I heard from God that way."

"You can and will. Let's try now." Lucas grabbed her hands, and they closed their eyes while he prayed.

"God, we love You and know You love us. We want to know if there's anything You want to tell us about our school year or about our lives."

Maria strained to hear anything. She waited and waited but only heard her stomach growl. She needed more s'mores. She opened her eyes to see Lucas smiling at her from ear to ear.

"What?" she asked him. "Did God say something to you?"

"Yep. He said He wants to show you what you were made for; He wants to show you your destiny."

Maria had just learned that when you hear something from God for someone else, the Bible calls it prophecy, and Lucas was prophesying over her! Her heart started beating really fast.

Just then, Harper walked back up to them holding her sister's hand. "Hey guys, did you hear God's voice? We had an amazing time."

Maria said excitedly, "Lucas prophesied over me that I am going to hear God's voice about my destiny."

"I know my destiny," Hartley declared, pulling
away from her sister's hand. "It's ice cream!" She ran

toward the cafeteria, because it was already snack time and the meeting had been dismissed.

Lucas looked at Harper. "Harper, let's pray for Maria that she hears God right now."

Harper agreed.

Maria thought ice cream sounded more realistic and satisfying, but she closed her eyes anyway. Harper and Lucas prayed for a bit, but Maria was lost in thought. She was imagining the worship time from earlier and how good it felt to sing to God about her love for Him. He was so good. She could picture a gentle father's face smiling from somewhere inside of her. She was lost in the goodness of the moment when she was shocked that somewhere inside her heart and mind she heard: "I have made you to be creative like Me. You are an actress." She gasped.

"What did you see or hear?" asked Lucas excitedly.

"I . . . I don't want to say." The words had been so clear; they had sounded almost like her voice but one step past her voice. She explained to Lucas and Harper how she had been caught up in thoughts about God when she felt she heard something, but she was still unsure.

"God speaks in all kinds of ways, and what you're describing sounds like one of those ways to me. I can totally relate," said Harper. "What did He tell you?"

Maria felt that if she told them, they might laugh at her. She had always loved acting and plays, but to do this as a career seemed too big. She looked at her friends and knew they loved her, so she took in a big breath and then let the words rush out: "I feel like He said I was going to be an actress."

Then Lucas said, "While you heard you were going to be an actress, I felt like I heard the word 'brother' over myself. We are hearing God!"

"Ooh, maybe your mom is going to have a baby," Maria said excitedly. She'd always wanted her mom to have another baby, but her mom and dad were happy with two kids.

"Well," said Lucas. "Mom and Dad can't have any more kids; they just had me and my brother. My brother was the last one, and they would have told me, I think. Maybe God is going to heal them. I don't know. Sometimes God tells you things that aren't what you would normally think. They're like hints, so when they happen, you say, 'Oh wow! God did that!' and you totally know it's Him."

The three of them had a quiet moment. Maria felt like she'd just had a computer update in her heart, one that filled her up with anticipation and answered some of the questions she'd had about her life and future. "I am an actress," she whispered to herself, trying on the word. Actress. It fit really well.

CHAPTER

2

Lucas walked into his house carrying a mountain of stuff—a sleeping bag, pillow, huge backpack, bag of soccer balls, his book bag—it was a never-ending pile. Maria's family had left town, so Lucas's family was watching their little Boston terrier, who was dancing at his feet, wanting attention and barking excitedly as if he had been gone for ten years.

"Hi, Jarvis." He petted what he called "the circus dog." "Mom, I'm home!" he shouted.

His two-year-old brother ran to the living room first and hugged Lucas's leg, demanding to be dragged around. His mom followed and gave Lucas a big hug.

"Oh, my little man, I missed you so much!"

He felt like his little brother for a second because of the way she hugged him.

"How was camp? Was it fun? Did you make any new friends?" She asked so many questions at once that he was almost dizzy. He loved being home though.

His mom was cooking dinner, so they all moved into the kitchen. He sat on the barstool by the counter, and his little brother pretended that Lucas's legs were the tracks for the toy train he held. Jarvis dropped his ball lovingly on the floor too many times, trying to get Lucas's attention too.

Lucas talked while his mom put potatoes in the oven and then started chopping up tomatoes and cucumbers for a salad. He loved telling her how his team won first place in the camp games. Games and sports were his favorite things, and he was usually the star and reason his teams won, but he left that part out every time. He knew his mom and dad knew it, though, and that they were proud.

Mom lifted the lid of the slow cooker and looked at the chicken before looking at him excitedly again. "What did God do?"

Lucas shared happily about the worship and the children's teams teaching, but also about a highlight of his week. "Right at the end of worship one night, the guest speaker, Shawn Bolz, got up and said, 'God is going to teach many of you about His love nature. He is going to give many of you an opportunity to show great compassion and to learn what that word means.' Then Mr. Bolz pointed at me and said, 'God wants to teach you how to love people like He does, and in soccer this year, you will have the opportunity to be a champion of compassion. Not only will you be compassionate, but you will help others have a compassionate nature.'"

His mom smiled. "That is beautiful. Did he know soccer is your life?"

Lucas got up and took some knives and forks out of the cutlery drawer. He knew how much his mom appreciated his help at dinnertime, and he wanted to set the table. "No, he was a guest speaker-type person; he didn't know any of us! Anyway, every time I was in worship after that, I felt like when you or Dad hugs me, and it made me almost want to cry. It felt so . . . intense, but good." Lucas thought for a second about the other thing God had told him about a brother, but decided to keep that to himself because he didn't know if his parents wanted to have more kids or not, and it felt weird to say it.

His mom hugged him. "I love that, honey. It sounds like God is going to make a great big deposit of something really special inside of you, and it's already started. You are so special."

The moment would have been special too if his

little brother hadn't been shoving his extra train into

his stomach to get him to play, and if Jarvis wasn't pulling on his shoelaces.

When he went to bed that night, he prayed, "Jesus, I want to know what compassion really means, and I want to love everyone like You love them." He felt satisfied with that and dozed off.

CHAPTER 3

"Sorry, Maria, the drama class you want to take at the community theater is full. You will just have to wait," Maria's dad said as they opened the car doors and got in.

Maria couldn't understand. She had prayed and asked God for a word about this year and heard she was an actress, but then there wasn't any opportunity. It didn't make sense!

"School will have some acting opportunities at some point this year. Remember the nutrition play you did last year? You were the cutest singing carrot." Trust her mom to bring up one of the most embarrassing moments of her life . . .

"At school everyone is in plays. It's sort of fun, but it's not real acting." Maria frowned.

Jarvis had ridden with them and now climbed up in her lap to comfort her. She pet him intently, thinking while her dad's favorite Mexican group played in the background.

"Honey, sometimes God shows you things but then there is an obstacle and you have to hear His voice again. If it really is God, He will make a way." Maria's mom reached back and patted her knee.

I don't think . . . maybe I didn't really hear God, Maria thought to herself. She had felt so strongly about it that now she didn't want to let it go, but it seemed like an impossible dream.

"Oh *hija*, tell God that you're sad and ask Him to work it out for you. He wants what we want more than we want it, because He wanted it first. When He spoke to you, you only caught up to what He already wants. If it's Him, He will help you—no doubt about it."

Maria thought about that. Did God want it as much as she did? She had already imagined herself in amazing plays as a lead actress, commanding the audience with her wonderful, God-given skill. How was she going to develop into that picture of herself if she couldn't even take an acting class? She closed her eyes and prayed out loud, "God, if You want this more than I do, please make a way for it. Amen."

Just then, the phone rang. Maria could

hear Harper's mom's voice on the line. The mothers chatted for a while, and Maria wondered if it was about the Friday night sleepover she and Harper had planned together.

Maria's mom ended the call and turned to her. "Nena, how about a kids' choir class instead? Harper's Mom just told me that Harper joined a kids' show choir, and it's at the theater we just left. That would be fun!"

Maria knew her mom was trying to raise her hopes, and it did sound like it could be fun, but it wasn't the thing she wanted most. "I guess so, Mamá. I

love singing with Harper." She tried to sound encouraged.

Her mom smiled and said, "I'll stop back by tomorrow and sign you up."

That night, Maria was sitting comfily with her dad's tablet on her bed, chatting virtually with Lucas and Harper. She loved social media, and Lucas was pointing the girls to all kinds of funny memes about PE class because Maria hated PE. Harper and Lucas always made fun of her for hating what

was, for them, the easiest class. Jarvis was snuggled up next to her, looking at the tablet as if he were part of the conversation.

After a bunch of small talk, Lucas said, "Let's practice prophesying. We can try to get words of knowledge for people. I'll think of someone I know really well, and you girls ask God to tell you things He knows about them. It'll be like we are praying for their lives when they aren't even here, but we don't have to worry if we don't get all the right prophetic words, and we can all take a turn."

Harper's massive grin made it easy to see what she thought about the idea, but Maria hung her head and sighed.

Harper could tell Maria was nervous, especially after hearing the news about her acting classes not happening, and she said, "Come on, what do you have to lose? It's just us."

So they all began to get really quiet. Harper crinkled her forehead on her tablet screen, and it made Maria quietly smirk at how hard Harper was trying.

"Is it a girl?" Harper asked Lucas.

"It is!" Lucas gave her a big grin.

"Well, we have a fifty-fifty chance if it's a boy or a girl," Maria said dryly.

Harper gave her a disapproving look but tried another: "Is she known for her kind heart and cooking?" she asked.

"Yes and yes!" Lucas said.

Harper pounded her fist in the air twice. "Yeah, team Jesus!"

They laughed and Jarvis barked at the commotion, rolling his ball toward Maria because he wanted to be part of the action.

"Is she in her thirties?" Harper asked.

"Nope." Lucas said. "How about you, Maria? Anything?"

Maria really tried to concentrate. She thought about this mystery woman and tried to picture her in her head. She just didn't feel or hear anything. She remembered that at camp the children's pastor said, "Remember, just try to love with God's heart. He loves when you try to love like Him. If you try to be powerful or make something happen, you are missing the point." Maria reached out to God with her heart and tried to picture what God loved about this woman.

She felt something. It wasn't something she had been thinking about, and it didn't feel made up. She felt like the mystery woman had been really worried about moving and that she had been praying about it. Maria could feel God's peace for the woman and knew that she was going to be able to move somewhere amazing that was near her family.

"Maria?" Both Lucas and Harper were talking to her at the same time, trying to get her attention from their little separate video screens.

"Lucas, is she trying to move to be around family?" Maria rubbed her forehead. She didn't want to be wrong and sound silly.

"Yeah, Grandma is trying to move here, but she hasn't been able to sell her house!" He banged his forehead with the heel of his hand. "Oh duh, I just gave away who it was!"

"I knew it was an old lady!" Harper shouted.

Maria was so caught up with a sense of God's love for Lucas's grandma that she began to pray for her. "Jesus, I believe You are showing me that Lucas's grandma is supposed to move here and that You are going to sell her house. Please give her peace until then." Just then, she *knew* that God was going to bring someone to buy her house. She was so confident that she told Lucas so.

"Oh man, guys, this is awesome! Grandma is going to be so excited about our prayer time for her. You have no idea. I've got to call her right now." He exited the video screen as they said their goodbyes.

Harper looked straight into the camera on the tablet screen. "Maria, do you think that if God wants to help Lucas's grandma with her house, so that she can move, that maybe He is already setting up a way to make His promise for you happen? You have faith that Lucas's grandma's house will sell, even though it's not selling right now. Maybe you need

to have faith that He is going to make your prayer come true too."

Maria understood what Harper was doing: She was doing what good friends do—encouraging her heart.

Maria went to bed that night very happy, with Jarvis snuggled into her arms. God was working for her already, just like He was working to sell Lucas's grandma's house. They just had to be patient. She didn't even mind Jarvis's snoring.

CHAPTER 4

Soccer was starting, which meant Lucas's real life was starting. Out of all the kids who played on the teams, none of them could match his excitement for sports. When the last school bell rang, Lucas couldn't have gotten to the field any faster. After everyone got there, Jayden, the soccer coach, talked to them about the season. Lucas looked around at all the familiar faces on the team. He knew almost everyone, other than the kid who was the farthest away from everyone else. He was tall and skinny as a skeleton and had the curliest black hair Lucas had ever seen. This new kid kept looking at the ground and kicking it.

As Coach Jayden set them up for different obstacle courses, Lucas noticed that the new kid wasn't very athletic. He couldn't help but pray a little bit for him under his breath, because he thought about how awkward the new kid must be feeling. The practice was good, but Lucas barely enjoyed it because he felt so bad for how everyone was treating the new kid because of his awkwardness.

The first practice ended a little early. All the kids were waiting for their parents to pick them up. Lucas was juggling a soccer ball and hanging out with some of the boys. Coach Jayden was over standing by the water fountain, playing a video game on his phone, but pretty far from the scattered players.

Lucas was a little lost in thought, so he didn't see the new kid tripping over a small hole in the field and falling right into the biggest, and sometimes meanest, soccer player, Jeffrey. He heard Jeffrey yell at him though.

"Hey, what are you doing?"

"Sssssorry." The kid sounded really scared.

"Sssssorry? Yeah, you are sorry." Jeffrey pushed him onto the ground.

Lucas hated the stupid conflicts some of the other kids like Jeffrey were always starting, but this one was especially bad because this new kid didn't have a chance if Jeffrey sided against him. He didn't want to get in the middle of it, because Jeffrey was pretty popular and had the tendency of making other kids'

lives miserable. Plus, he didn't want to look bad in front of everyone by defending this new kid who seemed so different.

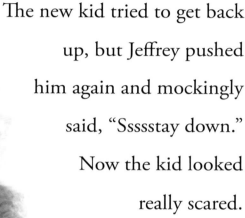

The new kid tried to get back up, but Jeffrey pushed him again and mockingly said, "Ssssstay down." Now the kid looked really scared.

For better or for worse, Lucas had to do something. He ran into the middle of it without thinking.

"Jeffrey, leave him alone."

"What is this, your girlfriend?" Jeffrey planted his face right in front of Lucas's.

Lucas turned his back on him and reached his hand out to the new kid to pull him up. The kid grabbed his hand and started to stand, but right then Jeffrey pushed them both down. A bunch of the kids started laughing when Lucas landed on the new kid.

"Lucas has a girlfriend; Lucas has a girlfriend," Jeffrey shouted.

Lucas got up and helped the kid up. He wasn't fazed by Jeffrey the bully, but the new kid ran toward the

restrooms, and Lucas thought he might have even been crying. Lucas looked at Jeffrey straight in the eyes. He was furious. He felt so bad for the new kid.

Jeffrey joined the other kids, who had already lost interest, and went on playing with the soccer balls.

Lucas walked toward the bathrooms. He saw the new kid by one of the sinks. "Hey, my name is Lucas.

Sorry about Jeffrey and the other guys."

The new kid didn't really look at him but said, "I'm Jamal."

"Jamal, did you just move here?"

"Yeah."

He didn't offer anything else, so Lucas tried to ask another question. "Where did you move from?"

Jamal shrugged and crossed his arms. "From all over. Last place was Sacramento."

Right then Lucas felt something pull on his heart. He felt the Holy Spirit surround him, just like He did when he was at church. He felt like Jamal was going through some hard things with his family and that God was asking Lucas to be not only a friend, but to act like a brother. Was this what that word about being a brother was preparing him for? To have a friend who was like a brother?

He felt a little weird, because he didn't even know the kid. It didn't hurt to investigate it, though, when he felt it so strongly. He knew he had to do something.

"Hey, want to come to my house to hang out after one of the practices?"

Jamal looked down at him. He was very tall. He smiled a little bit. "Yeah, okay. Okay, Lucas, I'll ask my . . . um . . . mom."

Lucas and Jamal were walking out of the bathroom when the circus dog, Jarvis, ran up to them barking. Maria and Harper were behind him, and they had just finished their practice too. Maria's mom had come to pick them all up.

"Hi, Jarvis!" he said. Jarvis ran after one of the soccer balls that one of the other kids had kicked. Lucas ran after him and scooped him up in his arms. He was thinking intently about what had just happened, and he couldn't wait to see what kind of friend Jamal would be, or what God would do.

CHAPTER 5

Maria's mom drove her and Harper from school to their new choir program. She was so excited to see what it was like. Neither of them had ever taken a class outside of school. It felt so professional to be a part of something that all her other friends weren't doing. Jarvis licked her goodbye as she got out of the car. He was as excited as they were.

When they entered the theater, they were filed into two lines on the stage—one for boys and one for girls. A pretty woman with a red streak through her blond hair made an announcement when they sat down.

"Thank you for joining our choir. This is going to be a very exciting time. How many of you have ever been to a musical?"

Harper stuck her hand up before anyone else. Maria knew she hadn't just been to any old musical, but a real one in New York. Maria had seen *Cinderella* in Los Angeles, so she was one of the other ten kids who had seen a musical.

"Well, you are going to be learning how to sing show tunes, which are songs out of musical plays called musicals."

Maria looked at Harper and whispered, "This is almost like being an actress!"

They both gave a whispered squeal.

A distinguished older gentleman in a suit and tie started to walk toward them from the back of the auditorium. He wore a long, wool scarf tied in a loose knot around his neck. "I am Mr. Wright, and I just retired in this community because my granddaughter lives here. I have taught music professionally for over forty years." He seemed very serious and professional to Maria. "My granddaughter runs this theater, and we are going to be doing a musical next season. I want to help train you children to be true actors, if you would like, so that we can put on a musical like this town has never seen."

Maria's heart started to beat fast. Not only had their town never had musicals, it had only had very limited short plays and small-time theater shows. She had looked it up. Now Mr. Wright had moved here, and they were going to be doing real plays that Maria had an opportunity to be trained for! She had goosebumps all over her skin.

"Maria . . . do you feel that?" Harper must have been feeling the goosebumps too. "I feel like I'm in a holy moment. It's your prophecy! God *did* speak to you!"

"Pinch me. I'm in a dream!" Maria said, and they hugged.

All the other children were excited too, but no one could have been as excited as Harper and Maria.

The class was extra long because Mr. Wright had each child sing alone. He said he needed to hear each child's singing ability so he'd know what to work on. Maria's mom must have been tired waiting outside because she came in and sat in the back of the theater along with a lot of other parents.

Harper stood at the piano, straightened her back, and tucked her curly, blond hair behind her ears. The music started, and she sang confidently. Maria thought she had a great singing voice. She'd heard it in church and during the karaoke they did all the time. She wasn't sure Harper would win a singing competition, but she could carry a tune and she loved to sing.

When it was Maria's turn, she was very nervous. She sang all the time at church and at home, but she had never tried to perform for anyone (except passionately in her bedroom when only Jarvis was with her). She didn't know how she measured up, and she had never even thought to ask herself if she could sing. She just assumed taking a choir class at the local theater would be easy and fun. Now she was super nervous.

She stood by the piano, and Mr. Wright played a note and had her sing it. Then she sang another, and it seemed to sound quite good. It surprised even her. Mr. Wright seemed to be enjoying playing a wide range of notes and having her follow along, sometimes playing a sequence slowly and others quickly. When it was done, the other kids clapped.

"Very nice, my dear," said Mr. Wright.

She was so excited. She felt like she was on the first steppingstone on the pathway to her destiny—until the last student went to the piano. Everything about her was perfect—from her straight, black hair and bangs to her perfectly pressed shirt and skirt.

A boy in front of them leaned over to his friend. "Her name is Brooke Lee. I heard she has been training since she was five."

Brooke acted like a professional. She stood like a grown-up in a ten-year-old's body, sure of herself and focused. She whispered into Mr. Wright's ear.

"Are you sure?" he asked.

She nodded gracefully.

He played a song from the historic Broadway play *The Phantom of the Opera,* and Brooke opened her mouth and sang with her flawless voice.

All the kids in the class were shocked. A few of them, including Maria, had talent, but Brooke was born a genius.

Harper grabbed Maria's hand. "This is amazing! I feel like I'm already watching a real musical!"

Maria's lower lip wobbled. It wasn't amazing or wonderful. Brooke had stolen the show. But God had given Maria a promise to act. How was that going to work out now? How many parts for kids would there be in this professional musical? Would Maria have a chance to even speak one word with Brooke around? She felt positively dreadful, but she tried not to show it.

That night, Maria's dad came into her bedroom with Jarvis and began to tuck her in. Jarvis jumped down and snuggled under her arm.

"What's wrong, Bella?" He used his nickname for her.

"Papa, I feel terrible." She told him everything. "Am I evil for being so mad that someone is better than me at what God has called me to? This is my destiny!" She cried onto Jarvis's furry back.

Papa looked deeply into her eyes. "My Bella, I know you feel God has called you to act, but why? Ask Him why, and He will settle your heart about this. Before you are ever called to be an actress, you are His daughter, just like you are my daughter, and that is your ultimate destiny." He hugged her and kissed her good night.

Maria sat quietly when he left. She decided to pray. "Papa in heaven, please forgive me for being so jealous. Will You show me why You want me to be an actress, like my papa said?"

Just as fast as she asked it, she saw a picture in her mind. It was a picture of all the other people in

the world who were actors, entertainers, directors, costumers, makeup artists, and scriptwriters. She just saw masses and masses of people. She felt a deep love for each person she saw—she felt love as precious as the love she had for her family. She began to cry again, but this time it was because she understood something that she had never known before. Acting wasn't her destiny; loving these beautiful people was her destiny. Acting was just a tool God had gifted her with to get to love all the other kids in the choir, the people in the musical, and even the teacher, Mr. Wright. She even had a deep love for her competition, Brooke. She could see how valuable Brooke was now, and she didn't care that Brooke was more gifted than she was.

Maria was so happy. She had never known that her destiny was love. She always thought it was to do stuff. She went to bed very happy that night and told her parents about her spiritual encounter the next day at breakfast. They were so happy with her.

CHAPTER

6

Lucas met Jamal at practice again. A few months had gone by, and being friends with Jamal was no easy task. He was extremely shy and would rarely talk to anyone else. When people picked on him, he got upset, and he was getting worse and worse. Lucas didn't know what to do. He had fun with

Jamal when they were alone together, but whenever they went anywhere else, it was like a chore to be with him because he never seemed to like anyone. Some of Lucas's other friends wouldn't even go out with him if they knew Jamal was coming.

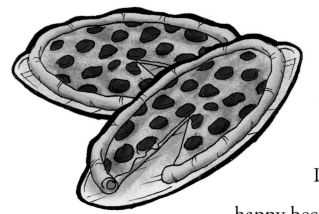

Jamal was scheduled to go home that afternoon with Lucas. Lucas was happy because his dad was getting out of work early to pick them up, and he had promised to take them to dinner, the video game store, and possibly an arcade. It was a real boys' night, and Lucas loved being with his dad.

Lucas went into one of the stalls in the boys' bathroom and prayed, "God, thank You for giving Jamal to me as a friend. Help me to love him well. Sometimes it's hard because he is not the easiest friend. Show me why this is worth it again." He felt guilty for asking God that, but he had to be honest.

When they hopped into the back of the car after practice, Lucas introduced his dad again to Jamal. Jamal barely even said hi. He was especially awkward around his dad, even though his dad treated him like he had known him his whole life. He would hug him and high-five him nonstop, just like he did with Lucas.

Lucas couldn't remember the last time he had had that much fun on a boys' night. He had even won a little stuffed animal that looked *exactly* like Jarvis, which he wanted to give to Maria. He felt almost

like he had the help of God on that one, because it was impossibly lodged into the display, but God loved that little dog at least as much as Maria did. Jamal and his dad treated him like he had won the Olympics.

His dad had made the night perfect, and he almost forgot how Jamal sometimes struggled to talk to other people, because he had seemed more relaxed around his dad. When they got into the car to drive Jamal home, Jamal was like a new boy.

"Thank you, guys. I've never done that before."

Lucas didn't under-
stand. "What do you
mean? Get pizza,
or go to an arcade
with your dad, or
buy video games?"
Lucas's dad had bought
them each a new
video game for their
handheld systems.

Jamal pushed his thumb against his chin and looked at Lucas. "Any of it. I don't have a dad. I haven't ever gone to an arcade. I've only been to a video game store once, and we don't get to get pizza very often, and never in the store where it's made."

Lucas's eyes got bigger. "Why not?"

"Um, I'm a foster kid. That means I live with people who help keep me, like temporary parents. It's okay though; the ones I have right now are really, really nice." Jamal pulled on his T-shirt and looked away, as if he'd said too much.

Lucas felt sad, but knowing about Jamal's life helped him understand Jamal so much more. He knew Jamal probably never told anyone he was a foster kid, and he was honored that Jamal had shared it so openly with him and his dad. It gave him a certain feeling inside that wasn't pity. It was a warm but sad feeling, and it made him feel more connected to Jamal.

What is this feeling? He squinted. Then he remembered his prophetic word at camp; he was feeling compassion! He was feeling a sense of understanding and consideration for Jamal, even though he couldn't relate to his circumstances or do much for him except love him. It actually felt empowering though, whereas normally he would have wanted to avoid the complex feelings that came up.

His dad changed the subject and talked to Jamal about sports, which Jamal knew a surprisingly huge amount about.

When they dropped him off, Lucas sat up front with his dad and fiddled with the Boston terrier stuffed animal. "I'm so sad for Jamal, Dad."

When they got home, Lucas's mom and dad sat down with him.

His dad said, "Son, God planned each one of us millions of years before we were born. We are supposed to ask Him for eyes to see that version of one another. I am proud of you for befriending Jamal; he needs a friend. He needs you and others to see who he really is, who God made him to be."

"I don't completely understand, Dad."

"Think of it like God looking at each one of us as though we are champions in sports. We have already won in His heart and we are holding a trophy in our hands. We all have that kind of value to Him, even people like Jamal who don't know God yet. God loves to show us His value for others, but we really have to look past some of their hurts and hardships in life, and even some of their flaws."

"Like how Jamal won't talk and doesn't know how to make friends?" Lucas asked.

His mom nodded. "Exactly. Think of it this way: If you see who Jamal was supposed to be when God designed him in the first place, you see past the flaws. What if you treated him like that? What if you spoke that kind of value into him?"

"How do I do that?" Lucas asked.

"I don't know, honey, but God showed you that you were going to grow in compassion. Here is your chance."

Lucas was determined he would do just that.

CHAPTER 7

Maria was taking Jarvis for a walk, singing her audition song to him under her breath. There was a starring role for a girl in the musical, and Maria had never wanted anything so badly in her life. She had to remember the words! It was audition day, and she wanted it to be perfect. Well, as perfect as she could make it, since Brooke was true perfection.

She was thinking about it all so hard, she totally forgot about Jarvis, who had been waiting patiently to get into the dog park they were standing outside of. "Oh, sorry, *cachorrito*, poor little thing; go ahead." She let him off his leash. He ran to play with all the other dogs without a care in the world. *Man, a dog's calling is much easier than a human's,* Maria thought, smiling at her little love dog.

A few hours later, Harper and Maria sat in the theater chairs waiting for their turn to audition. Mr. Wright wanted everyone to take a turn with the main song because there were plenty of secondary characters in the play, and he wanted everyone to have a chance to be on stage. Harper was humming under her breath in preparation, oblivious to everyone else around them. Maria was on the lookout for Brooke who, strangely, hadn't shown up yet.

Just then, a text came through on her phone from Lucas. His grandmother had sold her house! She was moving, just like God had told Maria. She was so happy—if God could sell that house and answer a grandmother's prayers, what was He going to do today for Maria? She hoped Brooke wouldn't show up and that she could be the star. She showed Harper Lucas's text, and Harper squeezed her hand excitedly right as Mr. Wright called Harper up. Harper did a great job.

Maria noticed Brooke coming in with her mom. She looked terrible. She was coughing loudly, and Maria knew she must have a really bad cold.

Brooke sat down a few chairs from her and whispered in a raspy voice to her mother, "I don't think I can do this."

Her mother asked, "Do you want to go home?"

Right then Mr. Wright called on her. "Can I have Brooke Lee up to the stage, please?" Brooke looked nervously around. She walked up to the stage and stood at the piano.

"Sorry, Mr. Wright, I am a little sick," she whispered. Her voice was crunchy and raspy.

"What was that?" he asked.

She tried to speak louder, but her voice wouldn't work.

"So sorry, Ms. Lee, but these are our only audition times. You can either take a moment to regroup, or you can go home and be assigned a secondary role."

Maria couldn't believe it. She wanted to stand on her chair and scream with happiness, but she held on to the edge of her seat tightly. Brooke wasn't going to win the role, because she was sick! God might have even made her sick so Maria could win!

Mr. Wright called Maria up. She had never been so ready in her life. She began to trumpet her song. It was flawless—not as perfect as if Brooke had sung it, but she felt good from beginning to end. The other kids clapped in a way they hadn't done for anyone else. She felt like a star.

Then she looked down at Brooke and her mom and everything changed. Brooke looked helpless and miserable, and her mom was rubbing her back while she tried to take deep breaths. Her body obviously wasn't working the way it was supposed to, and she was getting passed up for something that wasn't her fault. Maria's heartstrings pulled, and she suddenly knew that God would never make someone sick just to help someone else. She remembered what God had shown her about her destiny. Brooke was her destiny; to love her was her destiny, not to be the star of the show. Love was more important than this role. She went over to Harper, who flung

her hair to one side and gave Maria one of her "I'm a winner" looks.

Maria laughed but then got serious again. "Harper, do you believe God can heal Brooke?" she asked.

"Of course ! . . . Wait a minute . . . Are you wanting to go pray for Brooke to be healed?" Harper looked panicky.

Maria nodded.

Harper said, "Okay, I love that, but let's be realistic, just in case. If you ask her if you can pray for her and she is offended, or her mom is upset at you for bringing religion up to her, then you could get yourself in trouble, especially if they report you to Mr. Wright. Then he might get annoyed at you and you might lose your position, which looks like the lead role. Also, if God does heal her . . . you know what that means. You wouldn't get the star role. I love the way you think, and I am with you in whatever you choose, but you need to think through the consequences."

Maria had thought about all three of those things. The bottom line, though, was that God was giving her the calling and skills to act so that she would be in this environment and love people like Brooke well.

"I know that look," said Harper. "Let's go."

They smiled at each other. Maria walked over, with Harper following, and stood in front of Brooke.

"Brooke, I am so sorry you are sick. This might sound a little different, but we believe in the power of prayer. Can I pray for your sickness to go away?"

Brooke and her mom looked up at Maria from their chairs. Brooke had such kindness and gratitude in her eyes. Her mom seemed pleased that they even cared for her.

"Yes, please, I would like it if you prayed," she said.

Maria and Harper each put a hand on Brooke's shoulders and asked Jesus to take away the sickness because He loved her.

Brooke smiled at them when they were done and said a raspy thank you.

Maria didn't see any results but felt so much better that she had done the right thing. She really felt connected to Brooke and actually felt friendship chemistry that she hadn't allowed herself to feel before. She was so caught up in her thoughts that she didn't see Brooke go up to the piano. The next thing she knew, Brooke was doing her audition, and there was no rasp! She was the star—Brooke, the shining gift, not sick Brooke. Maria loved it.

Harper held Maria's hand and squeezed. "You are amazing."

Maria couldn't believe that God had healed Brooke. She was so grateful to Him.

After Brooke was done, all the kids clapped. Maria and Harper stood to their feet and clapped hard too. Brooke mouthed a thank you to the girls, and that's when they knew they had a new friend, but not just in Brooke. Maria had never known what being a friend *of God* felt like until that moment.

CHAPTER

8

Lucas, Jamal, Maria, and Harper were all waiting for Maria's mom to pick them up after school. They were becoming quite close to their new friend, Brooke, and she was having them over for a swim at her house.

Maria's mom was a little late, and most of the other kids had been picked up, except Jeffrey, who was walking up to them. Lucas dreaded even interacting with him because he was so mean.

Jeffrey flipped Jamal's hat off his head with one quick move. "What's up, girls?" he said to all four of them.

"Leave us alone," Harper said, standing in front of Jamal while Maria tried to pick up his hat.

Jeffrey kicked it into a puddle the sprinklers were running water into.

"Hey, man!" said Lucas.

Jeffrey just laughed.

Lucas wanted to hit him but knew that would do nothing. He also knew that if he didn't do anything, Harper might say a few mean things she'd regret later. What could he do? He prayed in his heart for God to help, not fully expecting divine intervention. Right then, he looked at Jamal, and he saw Jeffrey and Jamal as almost the same person. He knew he was getting a word from God. Instead of seeing Jeffrey as an evil bully, he could sense that he also had problems at home and probably struggled with his parents. God loved him too, and wanted to help him.

Lucas breathed in before saying, "Jeffrey, can I talk to you for a minute alone?"

Jeffrey must have
thought Lucas
was trying to bait
him into a fight,
but he looked
like he was game.
"Sure!" he said,
and he followed
Lucas over to
stand by the
bushes.

Lucas was super
nervous at first,
but he felt something strong in his heart for Jeffrey.
It was the same feeling he had felt for Jamal before
they first

became friends. Jamal was a foster kid who had some really hard things happen in his family. Because of that, he acted a bit weird around people, but he was getting better about how he acted around other people now—with the help of God and his new friends. Lucas didn't know anything about Jeffrey's life, but he felt like

God was telling him it was hard. He felt like he should show Jeffrey that he understood how he felt, and that if he told him about Jamal's pain, it would help him to stop being so mean to Jamal.

"Let's make this quick, loser." said Jeffrey.

Lucas wanted to cry, because he could feel that Jeffrey's bullying was coming from some deep hurt . . . but he didn't cry. "Jeffrey, I want to tell you a little secret and I hope you will keep it. Jamal has been through a lot of hard things. He doesn't live with his family. He has had to live in a lot of foster homes, and that makes him feel like he doesn't fit in. Have you ever been through anything hard like that?"

Jeffrey seemed a little shocked. He looked emotional, but he curled his lip and folded his arms. "His problems aren't my problems. What's your point?" he snarled.

Lucas swallowed. "You are making a hard situation even harder. I am a Christian, and when I looked at Jamal a few minutes ago and then looked at you, I felt like maybe you have had some hard things go on in your life too. God wants to help you like He is helping Jamal by bringing him friends. God doesn't want your life to be hard."

Jeffrey was turning red. "Don't judge me, Lucas." It sounded like a warning.

Lucas could see him balling up his fists at his sides, but he breathed in, hoping the Holy Spirit was backing him up, and kept going. "I'm not judging you. You were the one who was judging us. I'm just telling you that God loves you, and if things are hard for you right now, He can help you. I'm also asking you to leave Jamal alone, because he needs your compassion."

There were a few moments of silence. Lucas could tell that Jeffrey cared on some level. It was like God was telling Jeffrey how much He cared about him through Lucas, and Jeffrey couldn't come up with a sarcastic answer to that.

Jeffrey loosened his fists. "Fine, I'll leave him alone." He spat on the ground, right in front of Lucas's feet, and walked off.

Lucas felt relieved. He knew two things: one, that Jeffrey really must be going through some things at home but didn't know how to get help, and two, Jeffrey somehow was touched by the compassion that Lucas had for Jamal.

Lucas remembered the prophetic word he had received at camp: *You will be a champion of compassion, and you will help others to have a compassionate nature.* Even the bully somehow had a God moment with Lucas and backed off. Lucas had hoped that Jeffrey would have a more direct connection with God at that moment, but it was relieving that he had agreed to leave them alone.

Just then, Maria's mom drove up and the four kids jumped in the car. Jarvis made sure to give them an equal opportunity kiss. He even stealth-kissed Jamal, who'd said he didn't like dogs, but Jarvis was too quick for him.

Later that night, when Lucas was alone in his room, his mom and dad came in and sat on the bed.

"How are you, son?"

He told them all about the day and what had happened with Jeffrey.

Lucas's mom stroked his face. "I am so proud of you for your compassion toward Jamal. You have such a real love for him that your love influenced a bully. That is so amazing."

"Yeah, and Jamal is becoming so different now that he has been around you. You have treated him like a brother, and it is causing him to really change," his dad said, which encouraged Lucas. He paused for a minute. "Your mother and I have a question for you that could change our lives, and we wouldn't move forward unless you absolutely wanted us to."

Lucas looked at his mom and dad together. Was he in trouble? They both looked so serious.

"We have been taking adoption classes, because we felt like God told us we were going to have another boy. You know we can't have any more kids, so we've been talking about adoption a lot. We thought that the boy that God would give us would be a baby, but . . . as we got to know Jamal, we felt like we were supposed to find out if we could adopt him. We looked into Jamal's situation, and it turns out that he is eligible to be adopted. His current foster family can't keep him, and we've been approved to adopt him . . . if we want to. How would you feel about that?"

Lucas couldn't believe it. He remembered at camp when he heard the word "brother." He felt now that Jamal was like a brother, but he never thought it would be like a real brother. It felt so natural to say yes.

"Of course! Yes!" Lucas said. "Whoa!"

"We were hoping you would like this idea too," his mom said. "There are still a lot of steps we have to take, and we don't want to make it sound like it's a for-sure thing, but we are going to pursue it. In the meantime, we've been told we can foster him, and they said that if we're all ready for him, he could come live with us within the month. Would that be okay with you?"

Lucas was shocked, but he felt the presence of God in the room. Jamal was going to be his brother! He would have never even tried to be his friend or stood up for him

if God hadn't spoken to him about it in the first place. What a turn of events in his life, all because of his friendship with God.

CHAPTER 9

The girls had worked tirelessly on the musical, and now that they had a month behind them, they were closer than ever. Brooke, Harper, and Maria had become inseparable. Brooke had joined their friendship posse, and she had even given her heart to Jesus one night—at a sleepover with the girls. Brooke's parents had always believed in God, and had raised her to believe in Him too, but none of them had a friendship with God until Brooke learned it was possible.

Brooke asked to go to church with Maria, so all five friends went every week. Brooke's parents loved the little group of friends and the changes they were seeing in Brooke, so much so that they had even started attending church themselves.

One day, Brooke asked Maria and Harper to come to a sleepover the following Saturday night. She was going to meet a real casting director from New York and wanted them to be there with her. The casting director was friends with Mr. Wright, and he had seen the musical they had all been in. Maria was so excited. Now that she was Brooke's friend, she was no longer just thinking about her own opportunities but was in full celebration for Brooke's as well.

That Saturday night, Maria, Harper, and Brooke were talking in Brooke's bedroom. "Remember last Sunday when Pastor John said that we should include God in all our decisions, and that He wanted to talk to us about everything? I have been praying about what to wear and how to do my hair, but I feel like God is not talking to me. I know I can hear Him, like when I felt like He wanted me to give my life to Him, but this is one of the other most important days of my life and He is silent. Doesn't He still love me?" Brooke's eyes started to fill up with tears.

Maria thought about that for a minute. "Brooke, if you ask God something and He doesn't tell you His opinion, I think you need to see it differently. He wants to watch *you* choose. He enjoys you and your style. You are one of the prettiest girls I have ever seen. He probably loves watching you choose how you are going to do your hair and what you are going to wear."

Brooke sniffed and smiled at the same time.

Maria kept going. "He has put the Holy Spirit inside of you to help you grow, and when you figure out who you really are and what you like, and you make choices because you're happy being you, you make Him look amazing. Sure, God can tell you if it's significant for you to wear something that would make a difference for the casting director, but what if God is a good father who wants you to choose?"

Brooke looked confused. Then Harper added to what Maria was saying.

"Think about my little sister, Hartley. She is enjoying picking her own outfits for the first time. She picks everything, down to her shoes, and she is a good picker. Remember last Friday night—how proud my mom and dad were of her when she dressed herself in that entire princess outfit, with accessories, to go to the movies? We all loved it. Think about our Father in heaven who doesn't want to boss you around. He wants to help you learn how to make great choices, and He loves watching you make them. He gave us the Bible and His Holy Spirit to train us to be the best versions of ourselves, not just to tell us what to do."

Maria felt like Harper was being very wise, like a grown-up, and then recognized that the Holy Spirit was probably speaking through her, because the Holy Spirit is the best counselor in the world. She was touched by what Harper was saying to Brooke.

Brooke took a step back and tilted her head to one side. "So what you're telling me is that God doesn't just want to tell us what to do; He wants to help us be who we are supposed to be?" She reached into her closet and pulled out her favorite dress—a really pretty blue dress with frills and ruffles. "Then this is the one I'm going to wear to meet the casting director!" She emptied out her box of

earrings, picked two hearts, and then found a pair of matching shoes.

Maria looked at her after she was completely ready. "You look stunning. The director is going to love your look. You must make God so proud, because you make me proud. You've got this."

Brooke looked super confident as they all went to get in the car and go to the audition together.

After the girls and Brooke's mom pulled up to the right place, they all got out of the car at the same time and bumped into the casting director. Brooke's mom recognized him and said, "Oh hello, Mr. Jenkins, I am Cindy, and this is

Brooke. Her friends came for moral support." She winked at the girls.

"Delighted to meet you all. Aren't you girls wonderful? But let's see here." Mr. Jenkins looked at all three faces intently and smiled happily. "This might turn out even better than I thought. My next two appointments canceled and I need to cast three parts. Why don't you *all* come in with me and audition. You girls must be actresses as well, yes?"

Harper and Maria looked at each other in shock. They had only come for moral support, but the casting director had added them to their friend Brooke's casting audition. They were stunned into silence for a moment, so Brooke spoke for them.

"Yes, they are amazing actresses. We have all been in classes with Mr. Wright together, and they were in the musical you saw me in as well. We would all love to audition for you."

And with that, they went in and had the time of their lives. Maria felt like even if the audition was only a sign of what was to come, it was fun to just have the opportunity to do it.

A few days later, all three girls were sitting in Maria's room playing "keep away from Jarvis." Harper was telling them a story about how her mom lost her keys and how Hartley and Harper and her mom had prayed and asked God where they were. Harper had a word of knowledge about where they were—in a drain outside by the driveway—and sure enough, they were there.

Right then, Maria's mom came in. "Phone call, Maria," and she handed her the cell phone. She was smiling at Maria in a funny way, like she had a big secret.

Maria took the phone from her mom and raised her eyebrows at her.

"Hello, Maria, I'm Mr. Jenkins's secretary. I'm calling to let you know that you have been accepted for the role that Mr. Jenkins is hiring for. You'll be working with a commercial company. Mr. Jenkins said you were a wonderful actress, and he hopes to cast you again. I will give your mother all the information. I have already talked to her about this."

Maria looked up at her mom with tears of happiness.

Brooke and Harper were watching her with bated breath. They already knew the big secret, because they had both received a call from his office and had to wait for Mr. Jenkins to let Maria know too. It had been really hard trying to keep it from her!

Maria grabbed Jarvis and began to sing "You Are Good," a worship song they all loved. The other girls joined in, and although Maria had always known God was good, she had never quite felt how good until that moment with that song.

CHAPTER 10

The next day, Maria, Lucas, and Harper looked around at the other kids in kids' church. They had a few new friends now—Lucas's new brother, Jamal, and Brooke from show choir.

Jamal had gone through a night-and-day change

after going to live with Lucas. He was confident, bold, and excited about life. He also happened to be an incredible singer and had joined the theater with Harper and Maria. He didn't really like church though. He said that if God was real, He would have made Himself more obvious. Maria looked brokenhearted when he said that, but Lucas told her not to worry. He said Jamal just hadn't learned to see God that way yet.

They got to have a snack and social time before kids' church started, and Maria told the others all about Brooke's casting meeting and how amazing Brooke had done. Then she told them the additional news that she and Harper had also gotten small roles on a *real* TV commercial with Brooke. Lucas was so excited for them that he jumped up from a sitting position and about flipped over.

Harper smiled proudly at her friend Maria. "You're fulfilling your destiny of love so well," she said.

Hartley was sitting on Harper's lap and playing with Maria's little stuffed Boston terrier dog that Lucas had won a few months before. It was Hartley's obsession now, and Maria never got it back.

Their children's pastor started teaching that day out

of 1 Corinthians 2—about how the Holy Spirit searches the deepest parts of Father God, then searches the deepest parts of man, and ties them together. The pastor explained that when you are a friend of God, the Holy Spirit gives you downloads of God's heart and shows you things that make your life better and fuller. The friends all looked at each other and smiled. They definitely knew how real his words were, because they had all just experienced them.

The pastor explained that they were supposed to hear from God *and* feel what He feels *and* know what He knows. "Have you ever watched someone's parents or grandparents who have been married for a long time? Like my parents, they've been married for so long, they love cooking together, and the more they do that, the fewer words they need. If my mom needs salt, she somehow signals my dad and he hears it loud and clear without words, because he knows her nature and what it is to be with her and read her heart."

Maria felt that way with Harper sometimes, like when they were doing craft projects. She knew Harper more closely than anyone else in the world. They often felt like they needed fewer words but still felt like they were communicating a lot of things to each other. She noticed Jamal looking at Lucas while the pastor was talking.

"Well, God is this way when we have a deep friendship with Him. You just know His heart, how He thinks, and what He loves. It's like having inside jokes with your best friend, and when something is said, you laugh together. God is like this when you know Him well."

Harper held Maria's hand and squeezed. In that squeeze, Maria could hear Harper saying, "We have that. I love you. You're my best friend." It was just like what the pastor was saying about God.

"Lucas," Jamal whispered. "I feel that way about you. No one has ever, well, tried to get to know me like you, and now I feel like when

we go to bed at night, we talk a lot, but what we *don't* say is just as big, and sometimes bigger, than what we *do* say. You really tried with me, and I could always feel that you really cared. Thank you!"

Lucas looked like he was getting tears in his eyes, but he hid them and punched Jamal in the arm playfully. "You're my brother and I picked you out. I'd better care!"

The pastor continued: "The more we get to know God, the

more we get to represent His love nature to the world in a really natural way, just because we know Him so well. Who here wants to know God this way? Who hasn't met Him like this yet?"

Right then, Jamal raised his hand.

The four friends couldn't have been happier, and Lucas felt like he was dreaming. They all followed him up to the front

so they could pray for him with the pastor, and Jamal got to invite Jesus to be his friend that day.

EPILOGUE

The kids were all over at Maria's house. Lake Christian Summer Camp was due to start in a few days. Hartley was there too because her parents

were going out on a date, and Maria's parents had volunteered to babysit her at their house.

They were all in the backyard talking and watching Hartley playing ball with Jarvis, which was his favorite game. She always laughed to see him sprint almost as fast as a cheetah. She was so busy playing, she hadn't been paying attention to the big kids on the patio, but then the kids saw her look at them when she overheard Maria talking.

"Let's ask God for our next prophetic word, like at last year's summer camp. We don't need to wait for camp. God has been speaking to us so amazingly all year long." Maria told the others the full story of what had happened in one short year. "Jamal and Brooke, you two are an answer to what God told us last year at camp, and I have learned so much from you both!"

All of them seemed really excited to practice hearing God, and they closed their eyes, but Maria kept one eye on Hartley and saw her close her eyes too. Then

Hartley started smiling. She definitely just heard something in her heart. Jarvis gave her the biggest lick on the face ever.

"You're right, Jarvis! God loves us and wants to be our friend." She cuddled the Boston terrier.

Maria could feel Hartley's connection to Jesus. She was so amazed! Maria realized that God doesn't care how big or little we are; He is speaking to everyone He loves, and now she knew more than ever that God is the best friend they had. All of them had grown in their relationships with God in ways they could have never imagined!

PRAYER

You can pray this prayer if you'd like to grow with God too!

Father, You loved the world so much that You sent Jesus to die for the sins of the whole world—everything we've done wrong. Then You raised Jesus back to life to give us life.

I receive Your forgiveness and Your new life that You give me. You call me Your child, and I call You my Lord. You washed me clean and made me right with God. I don't have to feel bad anymore about what I've done wrong!

I welcome Your Holy Spirit in my life—Your gift of power for me to live a new life, like Jesus, and to have a close relationship with You.

Thank You, and I love You!

Amen.

About SHAWN BOLZ

Shawn grew up in a passionately Christian home with parents who were actively involved in his spiritual growth. Because of seeing how nurturing a relationship with God starts at a young age (Shawn and his wife, Cherie, both got saved at the age of three), he loves seeing the next generation empowered with tools that help them take their faith seriously.

Shawn is a best-selling author, conference and event speaker, TV host, and pastor in Los Angeles. Writing and telling stories are two of his favorite pastimes.

www.growingupwithgod.com
www.bolzministries.com

About LAMONT HUNT

Lamont Hunt is an award-winning character animator and illustrator, currently living in the Los Angeles area. He grew up in Springfield, VA, and Memphis, TN, but most of his growing up was done in the Sioux Falls area of South Dakota. He went on to gain a BFA in drawing/illustration/graphic design at the University of Nebraska-Lincoln. Go Huskers! He gained more specialized education in animation at the Art Institute International, MN; Animation Mentor; and Animsquad. Lamont has worked as an artist/illustrator and animator in South Dakota, Minnesota, Taiwan, and California; and with companies like The Jim Henson Co. and Ken Duncan Studio. *Growing Up with God* is his first illustrated children's book.

www.dakotakidcreations.com
www.facebook.com/theartoflamonthunt
Twitter and Instagram: @dakotakid76

GROWING UP WITH GOD
Workbook

An accompaniment for *Growing Up with God*, the children's chapter book, this workbook will encourage your kids to practice hearing God's voice.

Not only does this workbook teach children how to listen to God, it also gives them the tools they need to support and believe in themselves and one another. In each section that relates to a chapter in *Growing Up with God*, your children will find:

- A reminder of what was in the chapter
- A true story from a kid their age about how he or she encountered God
- Three important things to know about God's voice
- Bible verses to back up the teaching
- Questions for them to think about and answer
- A prayer
- Illustrations from the book to keep the content focused and exciting

This generation of kids will be the most powerful, prophetic generation yet, and this workbook is a journal and guide that will help them fulfill that destiny.

GROWING UP WITH GOD
Coloring Book

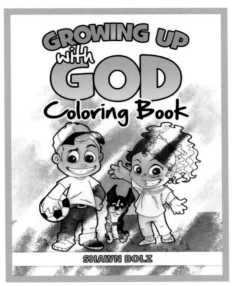

Growing Up with God has a coloring book!

In *Growing Up with God*, Lucas, Maria, and their friends spend the year on a journey of listening to God's heart of love. Through it, they learn how to support and believe in themselves and everyone around them. In this coloring book, your kids will experience the satisfaction of adding vibrant colors to the artwork of renowned character design and animation expert Lamont Hunt. Along the way, they'll be reminded of the life lessons shared in the chapter book.

This coloring book is awaiting your child's unique passion to color these characters to life.

GROWING UP WITH GOD
Study Course

Equip future generations with the life-changing tools
they need to grow into all God has for them.

CHAPTER BOOK | WORKBOOK | COLORING BOOK
TEACHER'S GUIDE | 10 DVD SESSIONS

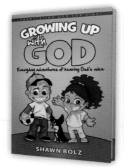  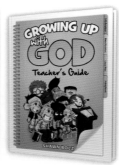 

Ideal for use in Sunday school, VBS,
small groups, and homeschool settings.

Parent tips included in each chapter!

BUY THE COMPLETE SET!
growingupwithgod.com